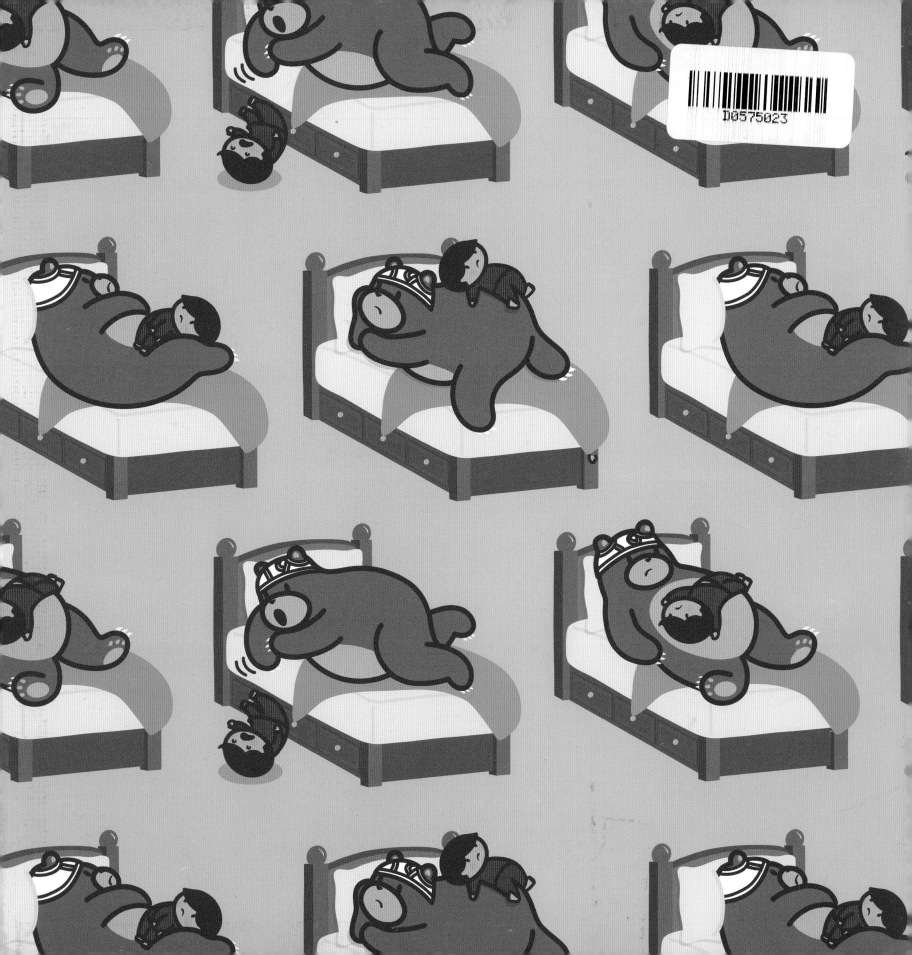

For all my fellow exhausted parents.

Hang in there!

—J.W.

Farrar Straus Giroux Books for Young Readers
An imprint of Macmillan Publishing Group, LLC
175 Fifth Avenue, New York, NY 10010

Color separations by Embassy Graphics
Printed in China by RR Donnelley Asia Printing Solutions Ltd.,
Dongguan City, Guangdong Province
First edition, 2018
1 3 5 7 9 10 8 6 4 2

mackids.com

Library of Congress Cataloging-in-Publication Data

Names: Wan, Joyce, author, illustrator.
Title: The bear in my bed / Joyce Wan.
Description: First edition. | New York : Farrar Straus Giroux, 2018. |
    Summary: A child faces the challenging task of putting a bear to bed.
Identifiers: LCCN 2017011503 | ISBN 9780374300388 (hardcover)
Subjects: | CYAC: Bedtime—Fiction. | Bears—Fiction.
Classification: LCC PZ7.W1788 Be 2018 | DDC [E]—dc23
LC record available at https://lccn.loc.gov/2017011503

Our books may be purchased in bulk for promotional, educational, or business use. Please
contact your local bookseller or the Macmillan Corporate and Premium Sales Department at
(800) 221-7945 ext. 5442 or by e-mail at MacmillanSpecialMarkets@macmillan.com.

THE BEAR IN MY BED

Joyce Wan

Farrar Straus Giroux · New York

What are you doing here?

Mooooooom, there's a bear in my bed!

Very good, honey. Let Teddy have his beauty sleep and come eat dinner.

No, not *that* bear!

I'll be back at bedtime. Don't touch my toys!

YAWWWN!

I'm back! It's time for bed.
Look at this mess!

First, let's put the toys away.

Then it's bath time. More like splash time with you!

Now we put on our pajamas.

Then we brush our teeth.

Now it's potty time. I said potty time, not party time!

Next, we read a story. We read books, Bear, not eat them!

Then we get into bed.

OW!

I don't think we can both fit in this bed. Unless . . .

Just about done! Now there's a bed for each of us.

A big bear hug.

Then a kiss
good night.

Now, let's tuck you in.

Finally, lights out!

Good night, Teddy. Good night, Bear.
Sweet dreams.

Is this what they call a bad hare day?